You're invited!

We pulled our bikes over to the shoulder of the road and waited until Bitsy screeched to a stop beside us. She took a deep breath. Then she blurted out one long stream of words in a high, quavery voice: "I-know-you-guys-have-a-sleepover-together-every-Friday-and-you-probably-won't-want-to-do-this-but-I-wondered-if-you'd-like-to-come-to-my-house-I'd-*love*-to-have-you — " Then Bitsy ran out of air, or courage, or both, so she stopped and blinked at us nervously.

"Well, since tomorrow was supposed to be Kate's night," I began.

"And Kate isn't going to be here," Patti went on.

"We'd love to come!" Stephanie finished.

Look for these and other books
in the Sleepover Friends Series:

The New Kate

Susan Saunders

AN
APPLE
PAPERBACK

SCHOLASTIC INC.
New York Toronto London Auckland Sydney

ISBN 0-590-43192-7

12 11 10 9 8 7 6 5 4 3 2   0 1 2 3 4 5/9

Printed in the U.S.A.   28

First Scholastic printing, July 1990

Chapter
1

"And here I am in front of the Supreme Court Building!" Karla Stamos announced as a fuzzy slide flashed onto the screen at the front of the room.

"*Where* is Karla?" Kate mumbled drowsily to me. I'm Lauren Hunter, and Kate is one of my best friends. She and I sit next to each other in the second row in Mrs. Mead's fifth grade at Riverhurst Elementary.

"The brown dot at the bottom of those steps on the left?" I whispered.

"There are nine justices — that's what the judges in the Supreme Court are called," Karla droned on. "They meet on Mondays, Tuesdays, and Wednesdays, from October through June."

Cli-ick. "This is me at the Jefferson Memorial," Karla said, as we blinked at a blurry brown spot in

1

front of another huge white building. "It was built in memory of Thomas Jefferson."

"Duh!" Stephanie Green muttered under her breath on the other side of me. Stephanie sits in the front row, but that day Mrs. Mead had asked everybody to scoot their desks away from the middle of the room, so they wouldn't interfere with Karla's slide show. Stephanie had ended up beside Kate and me.

As part of our social studies class, Mrs. Mead asks anyone who has taken a trip to tell us about it. Henry Larkin gave a really neat talk a few weeks ago about going on a fishing boat. But Karla's visit to Washington was putting thirty people to *sleep*!

Kate stifled a yawn. "Leave it to Karla to make even Washington, D.C., boring," she murmured.

"And this is the Capitol, with the House of Representatives on the left, and the Senate on the right. Actually, *I* may go into politics after I get my law degree," Karla added importantly. And then she clicked to another blurry slide of a lot of blue sky with a white streak in the middle.

"I don't think Karla's quite worked out the focus on her camera," I said in a low voice. I squinted to try to clear the picture up a little, and then I heard Karla say, "And here is the Washington Monument, built in memory of the father of our country, George Washington."

"I can't take this much longer," Stephanie muttered beside me.

"I wish she'd at least made a movie of the trip," Kate said. Kate'll watch any kind of movie: old, new, silent, musical, black-and-white, color . . . I guess even a *Stamos* movie. She wants to be a director some day. "Or a video," Kate added thoughtfully. Since she joined the Video Club at school, she's gotten almost as enthusiastic about videos. "I could do a lot better than this with a video camera."

"I know this slide show's not exactly the most exciting thing in the world," Stephanie whispered, "but to be honest, I don't know that you could do any better on video."

"What's that supposed to mean?" said Kate.

Stephanie shrugged. "Your videos are nice and everything, but you're not exactly Angela Marx. And that's who it would take to make a whole bunch of shots of big white buildings look interesting!"

Angela Marx does those fabulous rock videos for Heat, Hot Tamales, and the Jangles. Plus she looks pretty fabulous herself — she's the one in the leather micro-mini skirt on the new Chaz cover. "Of course, sketches might liven things up," Stephanie went on. She's always drawing. Stephanie's a really good artist.

Kate frowned and started to say something, but

Stephanie cut in with, "Lauren, what time is it? I think my dumb watch must have stopped!" She gave her watch a couple of thumps with her finger. "It has to be later than this!"

I stuck my watch under my nose to see it in the dim light. "Ten more minutes," I said.

"Worse news," Stephanie muttered gloomily. "It *hasn't* stopped!"

"Stephanie, am I going to have to separate you and Lauren and Kate?" Mrs. Mead said sternly. She was standing all the way at the back of the room next to the slide projector, but, as usual, she was definitely on top of things.

"Sorry, Mrs. Mead," Stephanie said sheepishly.

"Sorry," Kate and I echoed.

Somehow we made it through slides of Karla at the National Archives, Karla at the Library of Congress, Karla at the White House, Karla all over our nation's capital, until finally the three o'clock bell rang.

"Children, before you rush out," Mrs. Mead called over the noise of about thirty kids shoving their desks back into place, dropping books, stuffing homework into backpacks, and talking all at the same time, "Mrs. Wainwright would like to see Kate, Lauren, Stephanie, and Patti in her office."

Major bummer! Mrs. Wainwright is the principal

of Riverhurst Elementary School. She's a silver-haired lady with blue eyes and this icy stare that can practically turn you to stone! Patti is Patti Jenkins — she, Stephanie, Kate, and I are like the Four Musketeers. We do everything together, including get into trouble!

"Mrs. Wainwright?!" I groaned under my breath. I pulled myself to my feet in slow motion. I've spent enough time in Mrs. Wainwright's office to know I never want to repeat the experience!

"It has to be because we were talking in class. *Again,*" Stephanie said mournfully as the crowd swept us toward the door. "How many times has Mrs. Mead warned us?"

"Patti wasn't talking," Kate pointed out. Patti sits in the corner in the last row in 5B — she couldn't have talked to us during class if she'd tried.

"And I can't think of anything else we've done that would get us into Wainwright-type trouble," I said.

Patti joined our huddle just outside the room. "I'll bet she's mad at us for running down the hall yesterday, when we were afraid we'd be late," she said anxiously.

"Maybe," I said. We *had* clattered past Mrs. Wainwright's office, and slid into our desks three seconds before the last bell rang that morning.

"Don't worry, guys," Henry Larkin said as he went by. "I'm sure it's no big deal." Patti smiled at him — she kind of likes Henry — but I could tell she was still upset. Henry's a great guy, but he's spent more time in Mrs. Wainwright's office than anyone in the history of Riverhurst Elementary. By now he's probably used to it.

Stephanie wailed, "We're doomed!"

Kate squared her shoulders. "Well," she said, "let's go face the music." She marched bravely toward Mrs. Wainwright's lair. Stephanie, Patti, and I dragged along behind her.

To get into the principal's office, you have to walk through Mrs. Jamison's. She's the school secretary, and a very nice person. Usually, the worse trouble you're in, the quieter she is and the more worried she looks.

So when Mrs. Jamison practically *trilled* a hello, Patti said softly, "Either we're in luck, or it's so bad that she's trying to cheer us up ahead of time."

"Mrs. Wainwright is waiting for you in her office," Mrs. Jamison told us. "Go right in."

None of us exactly leaped for the door, but I was definitely the slowest. I can be brave when it comes to getting shots at the doctor's or camping out. But when it comes to school trouble, I'm a total coward. I was expecting the absolute worst! When

I finally walked into her office, though, I got a pleasant surprise. Mrs. Wainwright was actually *smiling*. "Girls!" she said as though we were her oldest friends. "Thank you for stopping by" — as though we had a choice — "I wanted to ask if you'd be free a week from Thursday to do my great-niece Lacy Nordstrum's birthday party. She'll be five years old."

All four of us breathed one huge sigh of relief. Unbelievable! Mrs. Wainwright wasn't on our case, after all. She just wanted to hire the Sleepover Friends Party Service!

Last fall Patti's little brother, Horace, had a birthday, and the entertainment — a pair of clowns named Ollie and Mollie — canceled at the last minute. Patti's mom had no idea what to do with forty screaming six-year-olds. So we came up with an idea to help her out. First, Patti dressed up in a tie-dyed T-shirt and glittery blue tights. She made herself some antennas out of pipe cleaners, a plastic headband, and Styrofoam balls. Then she painted stars and comets all over her face with colored sun block. She added a dusting of sparkly silver eyeshadow. And hey, presto! She was transformed into Sparkly — sort of a cross between a space alien and the Tooth Fairy.

I painted my face with black, yellow, and brown spots. Then I tied my hair into two dog ears and put on fuzzy mittens, brown tights, and a ratty fake-fur jacket of my mom's. Since I looked more like a large brown puppy than anything else, I called myself Barkly, the Party Dog.

It would have been embarrassing if anyone at the party had been older than six, but fortunately they weren't. It was going to be a once-in-a-lifetime thing. . . . So Patti and I actually had fun. We jumped around and acted goofy, and told all these incredibly corny jokes. For example:

Barkley: *"Woof! Woof!* What's the best way to get in touch with a fish?"

Sparkly: "Drop it a line!"

You get the idea — six-year-old humor. And the little kids absolutely loved it.

Only, as it turned out, the Sparkly and Barkly act *wasn't* a once-in-a-lifetime thing. One of Horace's party guests told her parents about us. Then her mother called *us* and offered to *pay* us if we'd do the same kind of thing at their house. And before we knew it, we were in the party business. Soon, Kate started taking videos of the high jinks, and Stephanie began coming up with party themes and favors, organizing activities, and making sure everything moved right along on the big day — sort of like our manager, which is exactly how she was acting with Mrs. Wainwright.

8

"We'd love to do it!" she was saying. "It sounds fabulous!"

"What time next Thursday?" Kate asked.

"At four o'clock," Mrs. Wainwright said. "Four until six."

"Is there a theme?" Stephanie wanted to know.

"A theme?" Mrs. Wainwright sounded puzzled. I guess she wasn't up-to-date on trends in little kids' birthday parties.

"Like dinosaurs, or cowboys, or the circus," Kate explained. "Kids like that kind of stuff."

"Like if our theme were dinosaurs, for example," I went on, "we'd tell a lot of dinosaur jokes and maybe stick little dinosaurs on the cake, and have prehistoric party favors!"

"Well, Lacy's mother is making the cake. But it's a regular three-layer chocolate cake, with fudge frosting," Mrs. Wainwright said with a smile. "So there's no theme involved there. But I'll check with her about the favors."

"And we'll come up with some ideas by Monday," Stephanie told her.

"Would you like any magic tricks?" Patti asked, because sometimes we bring along Magnificent Mandrake the Magician, also known as Robert Ellwanger, another fifth-grader.

But Mrs. Wainwright shook her head. "No —

9

Lacy's such a quiet little girl. A magician might frighten her. But I *would* like to have the party filmed."

"Kate takes care of the videos," Stephanie said. "Nothing wild. Just the *usual* shots of the kids singing 'Happy Birthday,' opening the presents, blowing out the candles, and cutting the cake."

"Right. As dull as I am, I manage that somehow," Kate muttered just loud enough for me to hear her.

"That sounds perfect," Mrs. Wainwright said, handing Stephanie a slip of paper with Lacy's address and phone number on it.

"Forty-two Deerfield Lane, at four o'clock next Thursday," Stephanie read. "We'll be there."

"Thank you, girls," Mrs. Wainwright said. "I'm really looking forward to seeing you in action."

And then she smiled *again* — I was sure it was some kind of record — and walked us to the door.

When we were safely outside of the school building, I asked, "Do you think she knows what our fee is?" We get between thirty and forty dollars a party, depending on whether or not we make a videotape, too.

"Who cares?" Stephanie said breezily. "We'll just look at this party as an investment in our future at Riverhurst Elementary! We'll do a fabulous job, and Mrs. Wainwright will think we're the greatest!"

"And if we do a bad job?" I said, because we *have* had a couple of failures. Like the time I got a little too enthusiastic with one of my Barkly cartwheels and knocked over an ant farm that belonged to the birthday boy, sending furious ants swarming all over the dining room!

"No way we'll do a bad job," Stephanie said. "We've done it plenty of times before. And we'll get in some extra practice at the Kennans' on Tuesday." The Kennans are my neighbors on one side, and we were doing Brian Kennan's sixth birthday in a few days.

"We're a team," Patti said, adding, "and there's safety in numbers — remember?" That was the slogan we'd come up with when we started doing parties with Mandrake the Magnificent.

"Yeah," Kate said, unlocking her bike and pulling it out of the rack, "we have nothing to worry about. If one of us messes up there are three of us left to bail her out, right?"

"Right," Patti, Stephanie, and I said.

Chapter 2

It *is* great having three best friends to count on, although Kate had trouble with that idea at first. In the beginning, it was just the two of us: Kate and me. We live practically next door to each other on Pine Street in Riverhurst — there's only one house between us. We started playing together while we were still in diapers. And by kindergarten, we were best friends for life.

That was when the sleepovers started. On Friday nights, either I would sleep over at Kate's house, or she would sleep over at mine. It got to be such a regular thing that Dr. Beekman, Kate's dad, named us the Sleepover Twins. Not that there's anything twinlike about the way we look — or the way we act, either. Kate's small and blonde, I'm tall, with dark brown hair. She is incredibly sensible, I have a runaway imagination. Kate's super-neat, I'm a world-class mess. Kate could care less about sports, I'm kind of a jock.

Still, as different as we are, we spent *years* together without ever having a serious argument. At those early sleepovers, we'd put on our moms' clothes and play Grown-Ups, or Let's Pretend. Cooking in those days meant stirring up cherry Kool-Pops in the ice-cube trays, and melting s'mores all over the toaster ovens.

But as we got older, our cooking definitely improved. Kate perfected her recipe for marshmallow super-fudge, and I invented my dynamite onion-soup - olives - bacon - bits - and - sour - cream dip. We graduated from dress-up to Mad Libs, and to our first, tame games of Truth or Dare. We also watched just about every movie that ever played on Friday-night TV. When there was nothing else to do, we spied on my brother, Roger, and his friends, or worked out ways to keep Kate's little sister, Melissa, from spying on *us*. And in all that time, Kate and I never had a major disagreement.

Then Stephanie moved to Riverhurst from the city, the summer before fourth grade. The Greens bought a house at the far end of Pine Street. Stephanie and I got to know each other because we were both in 4A, Mr. Civello's class, last year.

Stephanie was funny, and she knew lots about clothes and fashion. I mean, how many fourth-graders already have their own style of dressing, like always wearing red, black, and white? She also told great stories about her life in the city. I thought Stephanie was terrific, and I was sure Kate would like her, too.

Was I ever *wrong!* I invited Stephanie to a Friday-night sleepover at my house so they could get acquainted . . . and talk about your total disaster! Kate took me aside and said that Stephanie was a complete airhead. "All she ever talks about is shopping," Kate complained. And Stephanie told me privately that Kate was a stuffy know-it-all. My brother Roger probably came closest to the truth. He said they didn't get along because basically they were too much alike: "Both bossy and *very* stubborn!"

Luckily, I can be plenty stubborn myself, and I was determined to get Kate and Stephanie to be friends. All three of us lived on Pine Street, and with a little juggling, I arranged it so that we all rode our bikes to school at the same time. Once I'd gotten them used to that, I managed to run into Stephanie at the mall — accidentally-on-purpose — a few Saturdays in a row when Kate was with me. Then when Stephanie invited me to a Friday sleepover at her house, I said only if Kate could come, too. Then I yammered at Kate so much that she said she'd do it, just to get me off the topic.

At the sleepover, Mrs. Green made us a big platter of peanut-butter-chocolate-chip cookies, which happen to be Kate's all-time favorites. Then we watched three old movies in a row on Stephanie's personal TV, which softened Kate up even more. Finally, Kate asked Stephanie to spend a Friday night at the Beekmans'. And the Sleepover Twins were on their way to becoming a threesome.

Not that Kate and Stephanie suddenly agreed about everything, not by a long shot — to this day, they can be a little touchy with each other. And lots of times I find myself caught in the middle. Which is one of the reasons I was glad when Patti Jenkins turned up in Mrs. Mead's class this year. Patti's from the city, too. She's as quiet and shy as Stephanie is outgoing. Patti's also one of the smartest kids at Riverhurst Elementary, and definitely one of the nicest. She's also even taller than I am — a plus in my book because Kate and Stephanie are both shorties, and I was tired of feeling like the giant of the group.

Kate and I both liked Patti as soon as we met her. So, when Stephanie wanted Patti to be part of our gang, we said *yes* right away. Fifth grade had barely started, and suddenly there were *four* Sleepover Friends!

As the four of us climbed on our bikes and started pedaling up Hillcrest that afternoon, Stephanie went on, "This is probably the most important party of our *entire career!* It'll show Mrs. Wainwright what mature, responsible people we are. Not to mention talented and artistic." Kate raised her eyebrows at me. Stephanie can sometimes get a little carried away, and it looked like this was one of those times. "Let's try to come up with something different for a theme," Stephanie went on, "something special, not the same tired old circuses or cowboys or dinosaurs. And maybe we can beef up our videos a little, too."

Kate scowled. "Why?" I said quickly. "I think our videos are fine."

But Stephanie was off and running. "Tomorrow night at the sleepover at Kate's, we'll write down a whole list of terrific ideas for themes and — "

"Kate won't be here tomorrow night, remember?" I cut in.

"I'm going to that film conference with Ms. Gilberto and the Video Club," Kate reminded her. Ms. Gilberto is the elementary-school art teacher. She was taking Kate and the other Video Club members

16

to a weekend conference at the film center in the city.

"Oh, right," Stephanie said. Then she added with a grin, "How could I have forgotten? I guess Taay-lor will be going, too, huh, Kate?" She meant Taylor Sprouse, a sixth-grader that Kate kind of had a crush on for a while.

I said Kate was always sensible, didn't I? Well, even *she* slips up sometimes. Make that sensible about practically everything except Taylor. I admit, the guy is good-looking. He has straight, light-brown hair, which he leaves long on top and cuts really short everywhere else, a cute nose, and nice hazel eyes. And he almost always wears black. Pretty cool, huh?

The problem is Taylor thinks so, too. In fact, he's *convinced* he's the coolest guy at Riverhurst Elementary. Kate used to be one of his biggest critics. Then Taylor joined the Video Club. . . .

"Of course he'll be going!" Kate said crossly. "He's a member, isn't he?" She glared at Stephanie for teasing, and at me for grinning. But before she could go on about how it was really only Taylor's "excellent videos" she was interested in, someone called from behind us, "Hey, Patti! Lauren! Slow down!"

17

It was Bitsy Barton, pedaling like crazy to catch up with us. Bitsy's a girl in 5C who'd always been so timid that we'd never really gotten to know her. Then, on our last class field trip, to Silver Maples Park, we found out how neat Bitsy really is. She loves animals and knows all about them. She has tons of pets, and is always taking in strays. And she lives in a big old house on the edge of town that is absolutely stuffed full of her family — she has four brothers — and cats and dogs and all kinds of furry and feathery creatures.

We pulled our bikes over to the shoulder of the road and waited until Bitsy screeched to a stop beside us. She took a deep breath. Then she blurted out one long stream of words in a high, quavery voice: "I-know-you-guys-have-a-sleepover-together-every-Friday-and-you-probably-won't-want-to-do-this-but-I-wondered-if-you'd-like-to-come-to-my-house-because-Biff-and-Bob-are-going-to-be-out-of-town-with-the-wrestling-team" — they're her two older brothers, the ones in high school — "and-Barry-and-Billy-are-spending-the-night-at-my-grand-parents'-so-the-house-will-be-empty-and-I'd-*love*-to-have-you — " Then Bitsy ran out of air, or courage, or both, so she stopped and blinked at us nervously.

"Well, since tomorrow was supposed to be Kate's night," I began.

18

"And Kate isn't going to be here," Patti went on.

"We'd love to come!" Stephanie finished.

"Wow! Great!" Bitsy Barton squeaked. A large smile spread across her thin little face. "Is seven o'clock okay?"

"Absolutely," Stephanie said. "My dad will drive all of us over."

"I'm going with the Video Club to — " Kate started to tell Bitsy.

But Bitsy was so excited that she didn't even hear Kate. "I'll ask my mom to bake her quadruple-decker German chocolate cake," she said. "And maybe I'll make some chili-cheese dip, and get real taco chips. . . ."

I grinned at her. Bitsy was already planning the most important part of a sleepover as far as I'm concerned — the snacks! Stephanie and Kate tease me about my stomach being a bottomless pit, but I think of myself as just having a healthy appetite.

"So, we're all set for tomorrow night!" Bitsy summed up. " 'Bye you guys!" She turned her bike around and coasted back down Hillcrest in the direction of Red Creek Road, which is where she lives.

"A whole new sleepover menu!" I said. "I can't wait!"

"A new house, a new family — a total change!

This is going to be terrific!" Stephanie exclaimed.

Kate wrinkled her nose. "With all of those animals? Stephanie, don't you remember how much you hated the rat she took with her to Silver Maples Park and . . ."

"It was a *flying squirrel*, Kate. And I'd love to see all the different kinds of pets Bitsy has," Patti interrupted enthusiastically. She's practically as crazy about furry critters as Bitsy Barton is. "She has three or four dogs, and one of her cats just had kittens, and — "

"Besides, you don't have to worry about Bitsy's rats, Kate — you're going to the city with Taay-lor," Stephanie said. "Kate? Kate! Hold your horses!"

Kate had left Stephanie, Patti, and me far behind — she was tearing up Hillcrest and was already halfway to Pine Street!

Chapter
3

Kate didn't ride her bike to Riverhurst Elementary with us the next morning. Since the Video Club would be leaving on the bus as soon as classes were over, her mother had to drive her and her suitcase. So we didn't get to talk to Kate before school started. But she met us for lunch, and seemed pretty much her usual self, only sort of *quieter*. I just figured she was thinking about her exciting weekend in the city. Besides, Stephanie, Patti, and I were busy gabbing about the fun stuff we'd be doing at Bitsy's that night.

"Nana sent me a new curling iron — the kind that presses shapes into your hair. I'll bring that along and we can all try it out!" Stephanie was saying.

"Oh, yeah," I said. "I saw it advertised in *Teen Topics*! It does stars, and hearts, and zigzags." I'm always looking for ways to make my hair look a little more fun than its usual straggly brown self.

"Lau-ren, I can't exactly see you with a head of 'hearts'," Kate started to say, but Patti cut her off.

"I think I'll borrow my dad's Polaroid!" she said. "And bring along three rolls of film. I'll bet there'll be plenty of great photo opportunities at the Bartons'."

"Don't forget, we have to think of some themes for Lacy's party," I reminded them.

"Maybe Bitsy can help us out," Stephanie suggested. "She'll have a totally new approach."

"I think I'd better go check my suitcase," Kate suddenly mumbled. "Make sure I packed my toothbrush." She pushed her chair away from the cafeteria table.

"Don't you want your carrot cake?" I asked, snagging it off her tray as she stood up.

"Yeah, are you feeling okay?" Patti asked. "Aren't you hungry?" Kate had barely touched her tunafish on a roll.

"Not very," Kate said in a small voice. "See you later." She carried her tray to the bin in the middle of the room and dumped it without once looking back at us.

"She probably didn't eat much because she wants to be sure she doesn't feel carsick on the bus this afternoon, not with Tay-lor Sprouse around!"

22

Stephanie said as Kate stepped through the doors into the hall. "Hey, do you think I should bring my Heat cassettes to Bitsy's tonight?"

The Video Club members were leaving for the conference at three-twenty, from the parking lot behind Riverhurst Elementary.

As soon as Mrs. Mead dismissed us, Patti, Stephanie, and I followed Kate out there. Kate still wasn't saying much. And when I hissed, "Would you look at Taylor?" she barely gave him a glance. Just being cool, I thought.

Taylor Sprouse was leaning against the front fender of the bus that would take them all to the city, dressed entirely in black, as usual. He had on an old black sweatshirt, black jeans with holes in both knees, black high-tops, and a black leather band with studs around one wrist. He was squinting into the eyepiece of one of the club's video cameras. As we watched, he aimed it down at the ground, then tilted it up at the sky, and then started whirling it from right to left as fast as he could.

"Look at Mr. Hotshot Hollywood Director!" Stephanie giggled. I poked Kate in the back, but she ignored me. Then Patti said, "Here comes Bitsy!" We all waved as Bitsy Barton came walking across the parking lot with Judy Fisher and some other girls from 5C who are in the Video Club, too.

Bitsy helped Judy drag her big plaid suitcase toward the bus. Then she came over to us. "Mom's going to let us sleep downstairs in the basement," she said. "That means we can make as much noise as we want, and even stay up all night!"

"Fantastic! Then I *will* bring my Heat cassettes!" Stephanie said. "Plus I've just picked up this great new dance step from watching the Hot Tamales on *Video Trax*. We can try it. Their latest video is so excellent!"

"I haven't seen it. Oh, and I almost forgot," Bitsy said shyly, "please bring your bathing suits, too!"

"Do you belong to the Health Club?" I asked her, because it was definitely too cold to go swimming outside, and the Health Club on Main has the only indoor swimming pool in Riverhurst.

Bitsy shook her head. "No. We have a hot tub in our basement. Biff and Bob use it for their sore muscles after wrestling and football. Since they won't be here, *we* can use it! There's lots of exercise stuff down there, too."

"Wow! Just like at a fancy spa!" Stephanie said. "We'll take turns exercising and eating your mom's German chocolate cake, and we won't gain an ounce!" For Stephanie, *thinking* of ways to lose weight is as good as actually losing it!

"Attention, attention! Group, please line up in front of me so that I can check off your names as you climb aboard!" Ms. Gilberto called out. She was standing at the bottom of the bus steps with Mr. Kreski, the driver. "And please stack your luggage on the backseat as soon as you've carried it on, okay? Carly Anson!"

"Here!" Carly answered. She's a sixth-grader, and really cute. She has a heart-shaped face, curly blonde hair, and big brown eyes. She waved good-bye to a group of sixth-grade girls who'd come to see her off, and climbed onto the bus.

"Robin Becker?" Ms. G. was going in alphabetical order.

"Here!" Robin's a girl in our class.

"Kate Beekman?"

I turned away from Bitsy to tell Kate to have a good trip, but all I saw was the back of her best green cable-knit sweater. Then she disappeared into the crowd of Video Clubbers.

"Where's Kate?" Stephanie asked.

I pointed toward the bus. I felt kind of funny. I suddenly realized that Kate had hardly said a word to us all day. Was there something wrong? Then I shrugged. She was probably so focused on the con-

ference — and Taylor Sprouse — that she'd just forgotten to say good-bye.

That evening at a quarter to seven, Mr. Green
pulled into my driveway and honked twice. I piled
into the backseat of the car next to Stephanie, with
my cassette player — Stephanie's needed new bat-
teries — my backpack, and some copies of *Star
Turns*, our absolute favorite movie magazine.

"It's weird not picking up Kate, too, isn't it?" I
said as we rolled down Pine Street past the
Beekmans'.

"Kind of," Stephanie said. "But I'll bet she's
having a great time. She probably hasn't given us a
thought."

We swung by Patti's — she lives on Mill
Road — and then we drove out to Red Creek Road,
almost to the end of town.

That part of Riverhurst was all farms at one time,
and the Bartons' house was a real farmhouse about
eighty years ago. On some of our bike rides we'd
seen it from the outside. The front part of the house
looks pretty regular — a two-story wooden rectangle
with arched windows on the top floor, and carved
trim along the edge of the roof. But the rest of the
house is a crazy jumble of shapes, added on when

the different owners needed more room, and just hooked together. There are square additions with flat roofs, narrow ones with peaked roofs, and a small L-shaped wing toward the back.

We didn't have time to look closer, because Bitsy jerked the door open about two seconds after we got out of the car. She must have been hanging around a front window watching for us.

"Come right in!" she said with a shy grin. She nudged a big orange cat out of the way with her foot while she held on to the collar of a curly-haired white dog.

"This is Pumpkin," Bitsy said, introducing the orange cat, "and here's Whiplash."

"Why is he called 'Whiplash'?" Stephanie asked, patting the white dog.

"Biff named him that. Biff says he's been a pain in the neck ever since we got him," Bitsy explained. "But that's not really true. He's very sweet, and smart, too. He can do a lot of tricks. Whiplash, shake hands."

The dog sat down and offered his front paw to Stephanie so solemnly that we all started to giggle.

Bitsy gave Whiplash a quick hug. Then she called out, "Mom, they're here!"

We walked back to the kitchen to meet Mrs.

Barton. She's a tall, cheerful lady with lots of freckles and hair the same color as the copper pots that were hanging all over the kitchen.

We also met Mr. Barton. He looked kind of like an absentminded professor in an old movie. He was wearing old-fashioned wire-rimmed glasses, and he had gray curly hair that stuck out all over the place. He was kind of bashful, too, just like Bitsy. He was busy tinkering with an old radio in a little room on the other side of the kitchen.

"Dad's Mr. Fix-It," Bitsy told us once we'd closed his door. "He picks up all kinds of junk at yard sales and fixes it up."

"Then what does he do with it?" Patti asked.

"Oh, he saves it," Bitsy said, shrugging her shoulders. "It's all here somewhere."

And it *was*. There were old lamps, old coffee grinders, old toasters, old clocks, old radios, stacked on shelves in the dining room and spilling out of cabinets in the hall. If the Bartons ever wanted to, they could have the greatest yard sale of all time!

"Can you imagine a house less like Kate's?" Patti whispered to me. I guess she was remembering it had been Kate's night to have the sleepover. And, no, I couldn't! At the Beekmans', there is a place for everything, and everything's in its place. (That's one of Mrs. Beekman's favorite sayings.) But at the Bartons', every place there wasn't some old gadget or other, there seemed to be a cat, or a dog, or a cage full of chirping parakeets. Although I didn't see any rats. . . .

"Uhh, Bitsy, how many pets *do* you have?" I wanted to know. We were heading toward the basement stairs with Whiplash and Pumpkin tagging along behind us.

"Permanent pets?" Bitsy asked. "Um . . . three dogs, four cats, three parakeets, and a cockatiel in Mom and Dad's room."

"What about *not* permanent?" Stephanie asked.

"Well, Pumpkin's new kittens — there are four of them, already promised to people. Cats are easier to give away than dogs." Which is true. Didn't Stephanie, Patti, Kate, and I have a kitten apiece already? "The kittens are asleep in my closet upstairs right now. And then there's Mrs. Jamison, and her puppies."

"Mrs. Jamison?" the three of us squawked.

Bitsy looked embarrassed. "I named her that because she reminds me of the real Mrs. Jamison. You know, very friendly, with sort of reddish-brown hair."

"Better Mrs. Jamison than Mrs. Wainwright," I said. "Why isn't she permanent?"

"Well, Mom says we have too many animals as

29

it is." Bitsy sighed. "But the pound is just a few blocks from here and last week I saw a man taking her in, along with a box of puppies. They were *so* cute, and you know what happens if nobody adopts them."

Patti, Stephanie, and I nodded gravely. "No more Mrs. Jamison and family."

"So I told the man I'd take them all," Bitsy said. "Only Mom has said I have to find homes for all of them by the end of the week!"

"And if you can't?" I said.

"Back to the pound," Bitsy said in a low voice.

"Oh, no!" I murmured.

"Do you want to see them?" Bitsy asked.

We all nodded.

"Well, follow me," Bitsy said, skipping down the stairs.

Chapter 4

"*Ta-ta!* Here they are!" Bitsy pushed open the door at the bottom of the basement stairs. Out jumped a medium-sized wiggly dog with long reddish-brown hair and a plumed tail that wagged a mile a minute.

And behind her were the puppies. Three fat little brown-and-white fur balls came wriggling across the floor toward us. They were *adorable!* Patti, Stephanie, and I dropped everything we were carrying to scoop them up.

"Aren't you darling!" Patti crooned to the puppy she was holding.

"Hi, sweetie," Stephanie said briskly to hers.

I gave mine a squeeze and a kiss on the head, and he licked my nose with his short, bright-pink tongue.

"They're so cute!" I said to Bitsy. "I wish I could have one."

"Take your pick!" Bitsy urged eagerly.

"Unfortunately, we already have a dog," I said sadly, setting the puppy down on the floor again. Actually, our dog, Bullwinkle, is more like a moose. He weighs in at around one-hundred-thirty pounds. He's about five feet tall when he stands up on his hind feet, and he's practically my age, though he certainly doesn't *act* it. "I'm afraid Bullwinkle's too old to adjust to a puppy." *Not to mention too crazy,* I added to myself. Bullwinkle's idea of being affectionate is to rush at you going eighty miles an hour, knock you flat, and lick you all over. Somehow I didn't think a puppy would like that very much.

"And my father's allergic," Patti said, reluctantly putting her puppy down, too.

"I have enough trouble with the twins," Stephanie sighed. She has a new baby brother and sister at her house. "And more to the point, so does my mom." She paused and looked around. "Wow — check this place out! It's better than the Health Club!"

We were looking at two rowing machines, an exercise bicycle, a weight-lifting bench, one of those cross-country skiing machines, jump ropes, barbells, and a punching bag — you name it, Biff and Bob had collected it in the Bartons' basement! Clearly, they're as serious about sports as Bitsy is about animals or her mom is about pots and pans or her dad is about old gadgets. And then it hit me. Collectors — that's what the Bartons are! Even their *house* is kind of a collection of all these odd rooms. . . .

"How does this work?" Stephanie was saying. She handed Bitsy the puppy she was holding and jumped onto the cross-country skiing machine.

"Wait — " Bitsy began, but it was too late.

Both Stephanie's legs instantly shot out behind her, as though she'd slipped on a patch of ice. "Whoa!" she yelped, but then luckily she managed to save herself by grabbing onto the upright on the front of the machine.

"Whew," she gasped when she was back on solid ground. "I don't know if I'm ready for that one!"

"Try the bike, Stephanie," Patti advised. "Or a rowing machine. At least they're not going anywhere!"

I decided to check out a rowing machine myself. It was the kind that lies flat on the floor. You sit down at one end and brace your feet against the other. Then you reach forward to grab the oars and bring your arms straight back. Then the oars move foreward, and you go through the whole thing all over again. Once you get into the rhythm of it, it feels a lot like you're rowing a real boat.

"If I close my eyes," I said, "I could almost be . . . canoeing down the Pequontic." The Pequontic's the river in *River*hurst.

"Biff and Bob even have a video that you can watch while you row," Bitsy said. "It was filmed from a boat while it sailed across a lake, so you can pretend you're zipping along, with turtles and geese and ducks floating all around you. Want to see it?" She pointed to a TV and VCR on a raised platform in the corner. "Or do you want to have some snacks first?"

Was there any question? After all that exercise I was starving! "Snacks!" I said.

"Oh, no!" Stephanie groaned. "Watch out Bitsy — Lauren will eat you out of house and home!"

Bitsy giggled.

Still, everybody agreed, it was time for some food!

There was a small guest room on the far side of the exercise room, with twin beds and a fold-out couch. We dumped our overnight stuff there. Then we trooped back up to the kitchen. Luckily, the basement's under the main part of the house. Otherwise I had the feeling we would have needed a road map to find it again!

34

In the kitchen, Mrs. Barton cut us all enormous slices of German chocolate cake. And Bitsy heated up a big bowl of her chili-cheese dip in the microwave. Plus, her dad had brought home a large bag of real taco chips from Concha's, the new Mexican restaurant in town, and a carton of guacamole dip. We heaped everything onto trays, along with some Cokes. Then we carried the trays downstairs to the guest room, set them on a coffee table, and dug in!

The dips were great — we practically licked the bowls clean! And Mrs. Barton's German chocolate cake was *dynamite*. But I was so stuffed with dip and chips that I couldn't finish my slice. Whiplash was looking at it longingly. "I think he wants a bite of cake," I said.

"It's not good for him," Bitsy said seriously. "I'll go get him some dog treats," she added, running upstairs. She came back with a box of Milk Bones.

"Whiplash?" I said, offering the white dog one of the dog treats.

"Wait — he'll ask for it," Bitsy told me. "Whiplash — do you want a *treat*?"

Whiplash cocked his head, and when Bitsy motioned upward with her hands, he sat up on his hind legs, waved his front legs in the air, and barked one loud bark. It sounded almost as if he'd actually said the word "treat"!

"Very good, Whiplash!" I said, rewarding him with one.

"What about poor Mrs. Jamison?" Patti asked, holding out a dog treat to the reddish-brown dog.

"Which reminds me, you guys," said Stephanie, "what about Mrs. Wainwright? And the theme for the party?"

"Mrs. Wainwright's having a party?" Bitsy said, sounding a little confused. She was probably wondering what Mrs. Wainwright's party could possibly have to do with *us*. So we explained about the Sleepover Friends Party Service and Lacy Nordstrum's birthday.

"I don't know how you guys do it," Bitsy said when we'd finished. "I'd absolutely die of stage fright if I had to get up in front of all those kids and *perform*."

"I used to feel that way, too," Patti told her. "But they're just *little* kids. Anyway, after you've done it for a while, it bothers you less. I think it's actually helped me lose a little of my shyness."

Bitsy's cheeks turned pink. "Really?" she murmured, looking kind of interested. She was probably thinking she could stand some improvement in that area herself. "I bet you're right. But I don't have any talents."

"Jumping around and telling corny jokes doesn't exactly take — " I began, when Stephanie interrupted. "That's not true! Bitsy, *you* have a great act!"

"I *do?*" Bitsy couldn't have sounded more surprised.

"Sure! You have Whiplash, the Performing Dog!" Stephanie said. "He can shake hands, sit up and beg. . . . What else can he do?"

"He can tell you his age in barks," Bitsy said excitedly. "He can roll over, he can balance on a basketball — if he feels like it — he can . . ."

"Terrific! Why don't you bring him to Lacy's next Thursday?" Stephanie suggested. "It would be so great for us! We want this to be the best party ever, and kids love animals that do tricks."

Bitsy's mouth fell open. "I don't know if I could," she mumbled slowly, looking totally freaked out at the very thought.

Suddenly Whiplash barked sternly. He probably just wanted more dog treats, but it sounded as though he were telling Bitsy to take him to the party!

I burst out laughing. "See? Whiplash wants to be a star!" I said.

"Maybe I could manage it," Bitsy said.

"Please?" Stephanie said. "We need something

special, and Whiplash the Wonder Dog would really beef up our act."

"Well," Bitsy said bravely, "if it'll help you guys out, I'll . . . I'll do it."

Then we tried to think of fabulous themes for Mrs. Wainwright's party while we messed around with Stephanie's new curling iron. I gave myself a couple of zigzags across my bangs, and some more on both sides of my face. Stephanie covered her head with stars, and Patti and Bitsy made a string of hearts along the bottom of *their* hair. Then we took turns taking pictures of each other with Patti's Polaroid, to show Kate. But we didn't come up with any great ideas for Lacy's party.

"The circus?" Bitsy suggested.

"We've already done it," I sighed. "At the Reese twins', and Lindsay Osner's, and Timmy Fisher's."

"How about the Wild West?" Bitsy asked.

"Thousands of times," said Stephanie.

"Little kids love dinosaurs — have you done dinosaurs?" Bitsy wanted to know.

"Over and over again," Patti assured her.

So we gave up, and listened to some of Stephanie's Heat cassettes, while she tried to teach us the new steps she'd picked up from watching *Video Trax*. Bitsy kept forgetting the steps and tripping over her own feet. I guess that's because she'd never done much dancing before. Still, we had a lot of fun. But before long I started to get tired from showing Bitsy all the latest moves. It was getting late, too, and I began to wonder about the hot tub Bitsy had mentioned. . . .

I guess Stephanie wondered, too, because she finally stopped dancing and asked straight out, "So where's the hot tub, Bitsy?"

Bitsy called it quits on a crossover step followed by a low squat and a spin on one heel — the one Suzy Q of the Hot Tamales is always doing. "Oh, yeah," she puffed. "It's in here."

She led us back into the exercise room and over to the platform in the corner, the one with the TV and the VCR sitting on it. A video of a hot tub maybe? Bitsy lifted them down and shoved aside the piece of plywood that was the top of the platform . . . and *bingo!* It wasn't a platform at all — it was an instant hot tub!

"All riiight!" Stephanie said.

I stuck my hand into the water. It was really warm!

"You push these buttons" — Bitsy pointed to some switches on the wall next to the tub — "to make the water swish around. Either a little" — she punched a button, and the water in the hot tub began to swirl slowly — "or a lot!" Bitsy pressed another button, and the water bubbled and surged.

"It's like a geyser!" Patti exclaimed.

"Let's try Old Faithful out!" Stephanie said excitedly. "We'll put on our suits, okay, Bitsy?"

Three minutes later, all four of us were stretched out in the warm water of the hot tub, bubbles tickling our arms and legs and bursting all around us.

"This is great!" Stephanie said. "Remember when Kevin DeSpain and Marcy Monroe were at the country inn in *Made for Each Other?*" *Made for Each Other* is our favorite TV program. It's on every Tuesday at eight.

"Oh, right! I remember! There was a huge hot tub on the deck," Patti said. "Kevin and Marcy got in and — "

"Yeah," Stephanie broke in in a dreamy voice. "It was so romantic, wasn't it? Remember how they gazed at the stars and — "

"Stars!" Bitsy squeaked. "Hold on."

She climbed out of the tub, quickly toweled off, and ran upstairs. She was back in a flash, carrying what looked like a large, black, hard-plastic ball.

"We're going to play volleyball?" Stephanie asked doubtfully. She's about as enthusiastic about sports as Kate is.

Bitsy giggled. "Not even close. Just watch."

She set the ball down on top of her brothers'

weight-lifting bench and fiddled with a small black box attached to the bottom of it. Then she switched off the overhead lights in the basement.

"Wow!" Stephanie and I gasped.

"Bitsy, how beautiful!" Patti added breathlessly.

The black ball had hundreds of little pinholes in it, and a lightbulb inside. When the bulb was burning, light streamed out through the pinholes and onto the ceiling and walls. And it looked exactly like all of the stars in the night sky!

"It's one of Dad's gadgets," Bitsy explained as she slipped back into the hot tub. "It's supposed to be like the solar system — kind of like having a mini planetarium of your own."

"Look! There's the Big Dipper!" I said, pointing to seven stars in a group directly over the exercise bicycle.

"And the North Star," Patti said. "And the Pleiades. This is fantastic!"

"Yeah," Stephanie agreed. "We could almost be at that country inn."

"Or looking out at the universe from a space station," Patti said. She's a lot more scientifically minded than the rest of us.

"Hey, guys," I said suddenly. "I've got an idea!"

Stephanie stifled a yawn. The warm water was making everybody sleepy. "About what?"

41

"About Lacy's party, of course!" I said.

"And?" Stephanie asked, sitting up a little.

"What is it, Lauren?" Patti said.

"The stars! You know — like in *outer space?*" I said. "What do you think?"

"Excellent!" Stephanie exclaimed. Then she paused. "Do you think that's okay for Lacy, though? Mrs. Wainwright said she was kind of quiet . . ."

"I'd like to know what's quieter than outer space!" I said.

Patti nodded in agreement. "It's perfect! Lauren and I can do space jokes."

"We can try them out first on Brian Kennan," I added.

"And the favors can be little rocket ships, space monsters, or flying saucers," Stephanie said, getting into it.

"And Whiplash can be a space dog," I said, not wanting Bitsy to feel left out.

"Maybe you'd like to borrow Dad's star maker, too," Bitsy offered, meaning the black plastic ball.

"Dynamite," I said, flashing Bitsy a big smile.

"Congrats, Lauren, we've got our party theme! And now we can *really* relax," Stephanie said, sinking back into the warm, bubbly water with a satisfied sigh.

Chapter 5

The one bad thing about hot tubs is, if you stay in them too long, your skin ends up looking like it belongs on a California raisin. "Definitely not romantic," Stephanie said, examining her wrinkles before bed. "Do you think this happened to Marcy Monroe?"

But the next morning we were back to normal. We ate a big breakfast — French toast, cooked in one of Mrs. Barton's big copper pans, with wild-blueberry syrup. Afterward, Patti took pictures of all the dogs and cats in the house, *and* all their puppies and kittens. Then Mrs. Jenkins picked us up in her car and drove us home.

That afternoon, Stephanie, Patti, and I met again at the mall to check out Romanos for party favors.

Bitsy couldn't make it — she was busy looking for people who might be willing to adopt Mrs. Jamison and her family.

Romanos is a gigantic department store that sells everything from lawn mowers to mascara. First Stephanie made a quick detour to Aisle Three: Makeup, to look at some new patterned eyeshadow. But Patti and I quickly dragged her on to Aisle Six: Little Kids' Toys.

We cruised by shelf after shelf of talking dolls, wind-up kittens, and furry bunnies, and finally zeroed in on a scale-model rocket.

"Uh-uh," Stephanie said, after she'd read the information on the box. "You have to put this thing together. Plus, it costs nine ninety-five. Multiply that by the fifteen or twenty kids the Nordstrums will invite to the party, and you have a major expense."

"One-forty-nine-ninety-five, to be exact," I said. Math is my best subject.

Then Stephanie picked up a little robot that turned into a space capsule when she folded up his arms and legs. "What about this guy?"

"Perfect!" I agreed. "And it's only one ninety-five."

"I kind of like this space creature," Patti said, pointing out a little green rubber man with four pink tentacles and a removable helmet. "And he's only two twenty-five."

"That's a possibility, too." Stephanie took a little red notebook out of her tote and started making a list of toys and prices.

"And we should definitely get the Radioactive Blob from Mercury!" I exclaimed, pulling it out from behind a basket piled with water pistols. "See, just dump this little can of purple goop into the hole in his head. Then squeeze, and the goop oozes out of its eyes and ears!"

"Yuck! Please, Lauren! Do you want to gross out everybody at the party?" Stephanie groaned, pushing the Blob away and making a face.

"Are you kidding?" I said. "Little kids love this stuff, don't they, Patti?"

Patti nodded. "Horace sure does."

"Just wait 'til the twins get older," I told Stephanie. "You'll see. The more gruesome the better!"

"Spare me!" Stephanie muttered. But she wrote down "Radioactive Blob from Mercury" in her notebook.

We found two or three more toys that would make good outer-space-type party favors. And by that time I was hungry. I mean, I hadn't eaten a thing since breakfast, and it was almost two-thirty!

"What about some fries from the Burger Joint?" I suggested to Stephanie and Patti.

"I wouldn't mind a hamburger, myself," Patti said.

"Onion rings!" said Stephanie. "Anyway, we've got enough stuff on the list to give Mrs. Wainwright and Lacy's mom a few good choices." Stephanie closed her notebook and dropped it back in her tote. "Let's go!"

The Burger Joint has a long window across the front, which faces the center aisle of the mall. Their main griddle is just on the other side of the window. And if you aren't hungry before, you *will* be once you've looked through the glass. That day, the cook was frying burgers on one corner of the griddle, grilled cheese sandwiches on another, sausages, hash browns . . . My mouth was starting to water!

"Should we eat at the counter, or take it out?" Patti asked.

"Out," said Stephanie firmly.

Stephanie loves to sit on the bench outside the Burger Joint and scope out the passing crowd, which is what we did that day. We saw Todd Schwartz, this high-school guy who lives across the street from Stephanie, pass by with his girlfriend, Mary Beth Young. They were wearing matching denim jackets. Then we said hi to Sam Conti, one of my brother

Roger's best friends. We waved to Marcy Gitten and her mom — we did a party for them a few months ago.

And, in the meantime, we also finished off two orders of fries, one of onion rings, a burger, and a chocolate shake among us.

"I wonder what Kate's doing now?" I said, brushing the last remaining French-fry crumbs off my sweatshirt.

"Probably swooning over Taay-lor," Stephanie replied with a giggle.

"Oh, no, she's not," Patti murmured.

"What did you say?" Stephanie asked her.

"Look over there!" Patti nodded up the aisle to the left.

Stephanie and I stared at Duds, the new store for boys that had just opened. A guy with brown hair and shades was peering at the clothes in the window.

At the same time, Stephanie and I hissed, "Taylor Sprouse?!"

Then Stephanie shook her head. "It can't be. Taylor's in the city, remember? But who else dresses totally in black? *Nuts*! I wish he'd turn around!"

"It's definitely Taylor's hair," I said. "Notice how he's flipping the front part out of his eyes? Taylor always does that. And that leather wristband. It's got to be him! We didn't actually *see* Taylor getting on the school bus yesterday afternoon, did we? We left way before Ms. Gilberto got to the S's."

"I guess there's only one way to find out for sure," Stephanie said, scrambling to her feet.

"Where are you going?" Patti asked her.

"To window-shop at Duds, natch," Stephanie replied calmly. "You guys stay here. Three of us would be a little *too* obvious."

So Patti and I waited on the bench while Stephanie hurried straight up the aisle. When she got even with Duds, she veered off, and strolled casually over to the window next to the-boy-who-might-be-Taylor.

"I can't watch!" Patti whispered, covering her eyes with her hand.

"It's okay," I told Patti, "he's so busy looking at his own reflection in the window glass that he hasn't even *glanced* Stephanie's way. He's smoothing his hair back . . . now he's admiring himself without his shades. . . . He's putting them back on . . . oops! He's heading this way! And if that's *not* Taylor, I'll . . . I'll eat my French-fries container!"

"What if he sees us?" Patti asked anxiously.

"He doesn't know we're spying on him," I said. "Besides, we're just fifth-graders, which makes us invisible as far as Taylor's concerned."

I slouched down and gazed at my toes, but I was secretly watching Taylor out of the corner of my eye as he wandered up the aisle. He stopped every few feet to retie his sneakers, or fix the cuffs of his jeans, or move his wristband from one arm to the other, or grin at some older girls. And every time he stopped, Stephanie stopped, too. She was only about ten steps behind him.

Eventually Taylor moseyed right past us. Naturally, he didn't focus on Patti or me for even a second. And then Stephanie slid onto the bench beside us.

"It was him, all right," she said.

"Mr. Cool," I agreed.

"I wonder why he didn't go to the city with the rest of the Video Club?" Patti said. "I hope Kate isn't too disappointed."

"Or embarrassed! I mean, how often does Kate admit she *likes* somebody?" Stephanie added. "When we see her, we'd better not mention the city, okay?"

"She probably won't want to talk about it at all," Patti agreed.

And I said, "We'll just wait for her to bring it up."

I was sort of hoping I'd hear from Kate when she got back to Riverhurst on Sunday. But my mom dragged the whole family to a quilting fair in Dannerville. Then we went out to dinner at a Chinese restaurant there. We didn't get home until nine-thirty, which was too late to call Kate.

The next morning she was the last to show up on the corner of Pine and Hillcrest. Even Stephanie, who's always late, got there before Kate did.

"Remember," Stephanie warned us, "don't say a word about Taylor Sprouse."

"No way," I said. "Instead we can talk about . . . the sleepover at Bitsy's."

Patti nodded. "Good idea. I brought all the Polaroids I took. We can show her those."

"Shhh," Stephanie murmured. "Here she comes."

I turned to wave, and got the shock of my life. "Kate!?" I said.

What would you think if your oldest friend, who's never been messy in her life, shows up for school in a ripped-up navy sweatshirt, torn jeans — I'd never seen Kate *wrinkled,* much less with holes in her clothes! — and navy high-tops, laced halfway up, with their tops flopped over?! Plus a pair of dark, dark glasses, just like you-know-who!

"Hi, Kate," Patti said cautiously as Kate rolled up to us. "How are you?"

"Cool," Kate said from behind her new shades. "You guys ready to split this popcorn stand?"

What??? Kate sounded like a cross between Taylor Sprouse and that beatnik on *Ernie Wilson,* the old fifties sitcom on reruns on Channel 22. The kid who's always saying, "Cool, man?" I halfway expected her to pull a set of bongo drums out of her backpack and start thumping on them, the way he does!

"Uh . . . sure," Stephanie said, at a loss for words for once in her life. She was still taking in Kate's outfit, and I thought her eyes were going to pop out of her head!

"Then let's get in the groove!" Kate pointed her bike down Hillcrest, and coasted toward Riverhurst Elementary, leaving the three of us rooted to the corner like old tree stumps.

"It's a joke, right?" I said to Patti and Stephanie. "She's putting us on."

Patti shrugged helplessly, and Stephanie raised her eyebrows. Then we jumped on our bikes and raced to catch up with Kate.

Sticking to our original plan, Stephanie exclaimed, "Wow! Did you miss a great sleepover, Kate. Bitsy's house was terrific!"

"I took pictures of all of her animals," Patti added, rolling up beside Kate and pulling the Polaroids out of her jacket pocket. "See?" she said, holding a photograph under Kate's nose. "This is Bitsy's dog Whiplash. He does tricks, and she's bringing him to Lacy Nordstrum's party next Thursday!"

"Ummm . . . sounds far-out," Kate mumbled, before running on. "The video conference at the film center was boss!" Boss?! That's one of Taylor's favorite expressions, but I never expected to hear Kate use it. "It couldn't have been more supremo. I mean, like I learned all this really heavy stuff from the instructors there."

Patti nodded politely, not really knowing what she should say next, especially since we'd agreed not to bring up the conference.

But Kate wasn't having any trouble talking about it. "I learned even more about what makes a good video from the other kids, though. Like Taylor . . ."

Was Kate actually telling us that Taylor Sprouse was in the city after all?!

"Ms. Gilberto screened one of Taylor's videos for the head of the center. Taylor filmed it from a skateboard, and the center guy totally flipped over it!"

Yes, she *was!* Stephanie and I stared at each other, flabbergasted. *Was* that Taylor Sprouse at the mall on Saturday, or wasn't it? If it was, why had Kate made up this story? After all, *I'm* supposed to be the one with the runaway imagination! And if it wasn't, did Taylor Sprouse have an identical twin somewhere . . . or had Stephanie, Patti, and I completely *lost* it?!

"It WAS Taylor!" Stephanie mouthed to me. But that's when Kate checked her watch and announced, "Hey, gang, we better make tracks or we'll be late."

"Wow, you're right!" Patti said, thankful for the change of subject. She jammed the photos she was holding back into her pocket, and all four of us really started to pedal along. Being late means having to spend lunch hour in Mrs. Wainwright's office, which is enough to kill even *my* appetite!

We didn't have time to babble anymore since we had to absolutely race the rest of the way to school. But I was doing plenty of thinking. Like about Kate's clothes. They were Taylor Sprouse *to the max*, only the color was different: navy blue instead of black. The glasses were totally Taylor, too. Even Kate's hair was sort of like Taylor's that morning. Intead of parting it in the middle the way she usually does, Kate had parted it on the side. Classic Taylor Sprouse!

And not two minutes later, I had the real thing to compare it to. We weren't moving so fast on our bikes that I overlooked Taylor at the side entrance of Riverhurst Elementary. There he was, lounging against the railing, flipping his dumb hair out of his eyes. And he wasn't alone. He was deep in a conversation with Carly Anson, the cutest girl in sixth grade!

Chapter 6

There was no time to dwell on Taylor and Carly, though. We had about ten seconds to lock up our bikes and sprint up the sidewalk to the school buildings. "I hope Mrs. Wainwright isn't watching!" Patti whispered to me as we jogged down the hall.

"Did you see Taylor?" I whispered back.

"And Carly," Patti replied.

"Do you think Kate saw them?" I asked.

Patti just shook her head, because Mrs. Mead was standing in the doorway of our classroom. When she noticed Kate's clothes, she did sort of a double take. But all she said was, "You're cutting it awfully close, girls." And huffing and puffing, we slid into our chairs.

The kids in our class weren't quite so polite about the new Kate, though. During math, David

Degan hissed at her. "What happened, Beekman? Did your sweatshirt lose a fight with your washing machine?"

Kate just shrugged. Then Jenny Carlin, who's a real drip, anyway, murmured, "I thought Halloween was over!"

And Mrs. Mead finally had to ask Kate if her eyes were bothering her, because Kate actually left her shades *on* through reading!

That morning we had tests in science and spelling so we were too busy to find out anything more. But then it was time for lunch. . . .

"What do we talk to Kate about now?" Stephanie muttered to me in the cafeteria line. "What a great time she had with Taylor in the city, when we know perfectly well he didn't go?"

"We'll talk about Lacy's party," I replied in a low voice. "Let's not put her on the spot — not yet."

As it turned out, Kate was in the cafeteria just long enough to hear about our outer-space idea and grab a hot dog. Then she said she had to go to the art studio to talk to Ms. Gilberto about the video she'd started working on in the city.

"I'll tell you about it later," said the new Kate. "It's going to be totally primo."

Totally primo. Stephanie, Patti, and I could hardly believe our ears. We sat down at our regular table and were about to discuss Kate's weird behavior when Bitsy Barton plopped onto the one empty chair.

"Hey, Bitsy," Patti said. "Have you had any luck finding homes for your dogs?"

"No." Bitsy shook her head. "I've already tried everybody in my neighborhood, too," she said, looking worried. "Plus my aunts and uncles, even my grandmother, but *no* takers."

"Why don't we ask on Pine Street?" I suggested to Bitsy. "Patti has pictures of the puppies and Mrs. Jamison that we can use as visual aids."

"That would be terrific!" Bitsy said. "Do you really have the spare time?"

"This afternoon after school," I told her. "It's Roger's turn to start dinner tonight so I'm completely free." Since Mom's gone back to work full-time, Roger and I help her out by doing chores around the house. "What about you guys?" I added, looking around the table at Stephanie and Patti.

"Sorry, I can't do it today," Patti said. "There's a Quarks meeting at the high-school biology lab." The Quarks are a club for kids at Riverhurst Elementary who are really good in science. "And tomorrow's the Kennans'. But if you don't have any luck, Bitsy, I can help you on Wednesday. Maybe my mom and dad could put some notices up at the university for you." Both of Patti's parents teach history there.

56

"I can't today, either," Stephanie said. "The twins have awful colds. They were up half the night yelling their heads off. I promised my mom I'd watch them this afternoon, so she can catch up on her sleep. Also, Kate's coming by to pick up the video camera." Stephanie's dad bought us a video camera to use for the party service. We've been paying him back a little at a time out of the money we make. "She says she wants to try out a couple of things before the party tomorrow," Stephanie added, rolling her eyes.

"So it's just the two of us," I said to Bitsy. "I'll meet you on the front steps at three."

Before we left school, Stephanie, Patti, Kate, and I stopped by Mrs. Wainwright's office to tell her about the party. All I could think was, "Just wait until she sees Kate's *costume!*"

But Mrs. Wainwright was cool — she didn't bat an eye. She listened carefully to our outer-space suggestion and quickly looked over our list of possible party favors. "I like it!" she said enthusiastically. "And I think Lacy will, too. She loves the space show at the museum in the city. I'll give this list to her mother, and that should take care of everything. Girls, I am very impressed. You've done an excellent job."

Stephanie grinned proudly at the rest of us.

"Oh, and about the videotape. I'm most anxious to send a copy to Lacy's grandfather in California," Mrs. Wainwright added. "So I hope it will be clear, and properly focused. I've seen so many terrible home videos. . . ."

"I've never had a complaint," Kate assured her. "I've just been to a conference at the film center and learned all sorts of new things." At least she sounded like the same old Kate.

"Yes, I see," Mrs. Wainwright said, with a ghost of a smile. "Then I'll expect you all at four on Thursday."

"Oh, I almost forgot — " I stuck in, "Bitsy Barton will be coming with her trick dog, Whiplash, if that's all right with you, Mrs. Wainwright."

"That's a great idea," Mrs. Wainwright said. "Lacy is wild about animals. I'm sure she'll be delighted."

We were hurrying through Mrs. Jamison's office to the door when some of the Polaroids slipped out of Patti's jacket pocket.

"Let me help you," Mrs. Jamison said, leaning out of her desk chair to pick them up. "What a pretty dog," she exclaimed. "What's its name?"

Patti took a quick look at the photograph Mrs. Jamison was holding and blushed. "Uh . . . its name is . . ."

I came to the rescue. "Her name is Mrs. Jamison," I said, kind of apologetically. "Because of her color."

The original Mrs. Jamison laughed, and we told her about Bitsy and the pound and how we only had five more days to find all four dogs good homes.

Mrs. Jamison frowned and shook her head. "I can't understand how anybody could have abandoned four such lovely animals. I'd take one myself, but I have two dogs already!"

"That's what everybody says," Patti murmured sadly.

Since Bitsy Barton rode to Pine Street with us after school, I didn't get a chance to talk to Kate. I was counting on Stephanie to get to the bottom of whatever was going on when Kate stopped by her house later. Meanwhile, Bitsy and I set out on our mission to find homes for Mrs. Jamison and her puppies.

We tried the Norrises first. They live right on the corner of Hillcrest and Pine. Mr. and Mrs. Norris have two little girls, Samantha and Lolly, and I was sure *they* would just love a fat, brown-and-white puppy.

But Mrs. Norris turned us down flat, although she was very nice about it. "These puppies look as sweet as can be," she said, studying Patti's Polaroids.

"But Barney doesn't realize he's a dog, and we don't want to shock him with the awful truth at this late date by getting another one." Barney is the Norrises' big standard poodle. "Why don't you ask the Baileys?"

The Baileys live a little further up Pine Street. They're an older couple with no kids. No dogs, either, and we learned the reason why. Mrs. Bailey has the nicest garden on the street, and she meant to keep it that way. "Flowers and dogs don't mix," she said firmly. "Sorry, girls."

And so we went on to the Martins' house. But the Martins have a new little baby, and Mrs. Martin is afraid of dogs, anyway, even medium-sized ones, so . . . no go.

"What about him?" Bitsy asked as we pedaled up the sidewalk. She nodded toward the two-story house on the far side of the Martins', where a thin, gray-haired man was busy watering his lawn.

"Uh-uh. Definitely not!" I said, not even tempted to sneak a peek in his direction. "That's Mr. Winkler. He's the crankiest man on Pine Street, maybe in all of Riverhurst!"

So we passed Mr. Winkler and went across to the Kennans', where Mrs. Kennan told us that dogs give Brian hives.

We ended up ringing practically every bell on the

street, without a single nibble of interest from anyone. Then we spotted Todd Schwartz in his driveway
at the very end of Pine. He was washing his old gray
car.

"Hey, Todd," I called out, "I guess you wouldn't
be interested in a puppy." Todd's this enormous guy
who plays on the football team, and the basketball
team, *and* the soccer team. What would he need a
puppy for?

"What kind of puppy?" Todd asked, dropping
his sponge into a bucket of soapy water and walking
over to us.

"What kind?" I whispered to Bitsy.

"Just plain dogs," Bitsy mumbled with a hope-
less shrug.

"*Cute* puppies," I said to Todd. "We have
pictures."

"You're Biff and Bob's little sister, aren't you?"
Todd said to Bitsy as he flipped through the Polaroids.
"Wow! These puppies are cute. Males or females?"

"T-t-two males and one f-female," Bitsy managed to stammer.

"You know what? I think I'll take a male, and
give it to Mary Beth for our twenty-third anniversary
at the end of this week!" Luckily he added, "Twenty-
three months," because I was pretty confused. I
mean, Todd is only seventeen years old, and sev-

enteen minus twenty-three years ends up with *minus six!*

"You will?" Bitsy yelped. "Wow! Thank you so much!"

"Oh, that's okay," Todd said, looking pleased with himself. "Mary Beth's going to love him, and I'm glad to be able to give the little guy a good home. Why don't you tell Biff to drop him by on Tuesday after soccer practice? I'll buy him a collar and a leash, and surprise Mary Beth with him on Friday night. I think I'll call him Butch . . . or maybe Tiger . . . or King!"

We left Todd trying out rough, tough names for the puppy and headed back down the sidewalk toward my house.

"One down and three to go," I said.

Bitsy nodded happily. "This is a great start. Now if Patti and I can just turn up a couple of people at the university, we'll be all set!"

"Maybe my mom and dad could ask at their offices, and Mr. Green, too," I told Bitsy. "And Dr. Beekman at the hospital." Although I wasn't sure about mentioning it to Kate, since she was acting so strange. . . .

Before dinner that evening, I got a call from Stephanie. "Lauren, it's me," she said. "Listen, Kate came over — "

"And?" I said eagerly.

"All she talked about was her weekend in the city!" Stephanie said.

"Did she say anything else about Taylor?" I asked.

"You bet. According to our friend Kate Beekman, Taylor's the number one video artist in the world!" Stephanie reported.

"Stephanie," I said, "maybe that *wasn't* Taylor at the mall."

"Listen, all we have to do is ask Judy Fisher if he went to the conference. Or Robin Becker. Or anybody else in the Video Club!"

"I don't think I especially want to know for sure," I said. "But it isn't like Kate to lie about it. Not the Kate I used to know, anyway."

"I know what you mean," Stephanie said gloomily. "It's like Kate's had a personality transplant!"

That made me feel kind of funny. I mean, how would you like it if your oldest friend in the world suddenly started acting too cool for words?

"Maybe she'll snap out of it soon," I said as I hung up.

Patti phoned me before I went to bed, with more news. "Dad drove Horace and me to Tony's Italian Kitchen for take-out pizza tonight, and guess who was sitting there? Taylor and Carly, in a booth with Mr. and Mrs. Sprouse! Poor Kate! She must really like him to be dressing like him and everything. . . ."

"You think this whole mess is about Taylor?" I asked.

"What else could it be?" said Patti.

I sighed. "I don't know," I said. "But I hope she starts acting normal again. I don't know how much more of this I can take!"

Chapter
7

I could have called Kate that evening, of course. But I didn't know what to say to her. The Kate in a ripped sweatshirt, wearing shades, and saying "cool, man" every three seconds just wasn't the Kate I knew. So I decided to wait and see what would happen.

Tuesday was Brian Kennan's party. That morning, Kate was late meeting us at the corner again, which was strange because Kate's never late. When she finally showed up, she was wearing a baggy white T-shirt under another torn sweatshirt — where was she getting these clothes?! — her denim skirt with only one pocket ripped off, and neon-green tights with squiggles on them. Plus she'd crimped her hair on one side and tied it with an old, purple bandanna. She was starting to look pretty freaky!

And we hardly got to talk to her all day. At lunch, she headed for the art studio again. Then she rushed off right after school, saying she wanted to "change" for the party.

I thought she meant she'd neaten up a little, but not at all. She put on those torn jeans again and another "new" sweatshirt, which was absolutely full of holes! And it wasn't long before we figured out why she hadn't wanted to wear her skirt.

The Sleepover Friends Party Service was doing the Kennans' party for free — except for all the cake and ice cream we could eat, of course — because the Kennans are our neighbors. They'd also just bought their house and were on a tight budget, and my mom and Mrs. Beekman said it would be the nice thing to do. Mrs. Kennan let us choose any theme we liked. So we got to try out the outer-space stuff we'd be doing for Lacy Nordstrum, and even more importantly, for Mrs. Wainwright.

Patti and I basically dressed the way we always do for our party routine. Patti added a few more stars and comets to her face design, because of the space theme. And I gave myself a bright blue nose. Why not? Barkly, the Party Dog from Jupiter!

And we stuck pretty much to space jokes, like:

Sparkly: "Can a Martian jump higher than the Empire State Building?"

66

Barkly: "Sure! The Empire State Building can't jump at all! *Arf, arf, arf!*"

Or:

Barkly: "Sparkly, what time is it when a flying saucer lands on your roof?"

Sparkly: "Time to get a new roof! Hee, hee, hee!" Sparkly has a high, tinkly little laugh.

We even told some totally dumb jokes, like:

Sparkly: "How can you tell a rocketship from a chicken?"

Barkly: "*Wooooof!* If it lays an egg, it's a chicken!"

Then we turned a few cartwheels, and I honked the old bike horn I hang on my belt and chased Patti around.

Usually little kids love this kind of stuff, but that afternoon we had a hard time getting them to pay attention to us at all. They were too busy watching Kate! She was putting on a pretty good performance, herself. With the eyepiece of the camera practically glued to her dark glasses, she'd aim the lens straight at our heads, or the kids', filming them from only inches away!

"This'll be totally far-out!" she exclaimed. "Close-ups will make everybody who's watching the video feel as though they're part of *the experience* — almost like they're at the party themselves!"

Then Kate stood in one spot, and whirled the camera around from left to right, and then right to left, just the way Taylor Sprouse was doing in the parking lot on Friday — only more so!

Stephanie finally asked her straight out, "Is that one of the video tricks *Taylor* taught you at the conference?"

"As a matter of fact," Kate replied, "it's a technique called panning."

Patti and I finished our Sparkly-and-Barkly act, turned out the overhead lights, and switched on Bitsy's star machine. Then Mrs. Kennan carried out the birthday cake. That's when we realized why Kate had changed into jeans. Mrs. Kennan set the cake down on the table in front of Brian, she lit the candles . . . and all of a sudden, Kate lay down flat on the floor beside Brian's chair!

"Kate, get up! What in the world do you think you're doing?!" Stephanie hissed. She looked as though she'd like to give Kate a swift kick!

"This is going to be a fab shot," Kate murmured. She aimed the video camera up at Brian from below. "This light is amazing! I'm looking right up at the candles, and his face — "

"You're looking right up his nose!" I muttered. "And the kids can't even remember the words to 'Happy Birthday,' they're so busy watching *you!*" It was true. Jessica Freedman was standing up on her chair so she could see Kate better. The Reese twins were crawling under the table to get an even closer look, and Brian was staring at her, goggle-eyed.

"Kate, if you don't get up — " Stephanie leaned down to growl in Kate's ear.

"Okay, okay! Chill out!" Kate climbed to her feet. "But I want you to know you've made me ruin a really ultimo set-up!"

Ultimo? I was starting to get a headache.

For the rest of the party, Stephanie, Patti, and I each had to keep one eye on the kids, and the other on *Kate*!

But that wasn't the worst of it. After the party was finally over and we'd all gone home, I was scraping off my space dog makeup when Stephanie called.

"I'm coming over, okay?" she announced grimly. "I've got something I want to show you."

"It's almost dinnertime, and I told Mom I'd make potato salad — " I began, but Stephanie cut in.

"This won't take long, and it's *very* important," she said. "See you in a sec."

She must have pedaled ninety miles an hour, because it wasn't much *more* than a second before Stephanie rang my doorbell.

"Wait'll you see this," Stephanie said, waving a videocassette under my nose. "I was so freaked out by the time we left the Kennans' that I forgot to take this out of the camera and give it to Mrs. Kennan," she continued, "and boy, am I glad! Where's your VCR?"

"It's in the den," I replied. "Come on."

We popped the tape into the VCR, and settled down to watch.

"Oh, no!" I groaned, peering at the screen in disbelief.

"I call it the Taylor Sprouse School of Fruitcake Filmmaking," said Stephanie wryly.

"I see what you mean!" I agreed.

There Patti and I were up on the screen. Or *parts* of us were, at any rate. Kate had zoomed in on one of Patti's comets, the one on her left cheek. Then on the brown spot around my right eye, then the horn on my belt, then Patti's antennas. Next she panned the camera across the crowd of kids, back and forth, back and forth, back and forth —

Ulp! "I think I'm getting seasick!" I said, gulping queasily.

Then it was time for the famous girl-on-the-floor routine. And the camera *was* pointed up Brian's nose!

"That's enough," Stephanie groaned. "I can't take any more!" She jumped up and punched the "off" button on the VCR. She slumped back onto the couch, and the two of us stared at each other, horrified.

"We can't give that thing to Mrs. Kennan!" I said.

"That's the least of our worries," Stephanie said. "Imagine handing one just like it to Mrs. Wainwright! We've got to do something about this, and fast!"

"Like what?" I asked.

"We have to show Kate she's acting like a goof over Taylor!" Stephanie said firmly. "I just have to figure out the best way to do it."

Stephanie's always coming up with amazing plans, some of which work, and some of which don't. But this one was a doozy! When I got to the corner the next morning, Patti was already waiting.

"Do you have any idea why Stephanie asked me to bring the Polaroids from Bitsy's?" Patti asked me. "And my camera, too?"

"It must have something to do with Kate," I said.

But I couldn't imagine what. Then Stephanie rode up with Kate close behind her. Stephanie just managed to stuff Patti's camera and pictures into her tote before Kate braked to a stop beside us.

That day, Kate was wearing her blue-and-white ski jacket (the old Kate) and some totally faded and baggy black sweats (the new Kate). I didn't know if that was a bad sign, or a good one. And I didn't get to talk to her at lunch and find out, because we'd barely gone through the cafeteria line when Stephanie scooped up her egg salad on a roll and whispered to me, "Follow my lead!"

Then she turned to Kate and announced, "Lauren and I have to talk to Mrs. Jamison!" Then we scooted off, both of us clutching our sandwiches.

"What are we talking to Mrs. Jamison about?" I asked her as we dashed down the hall.

"We're not," Stephanie said. "We're going to look for Taylor Sprouse."

"Taylor? What are we supposed to do if we find him?" I asked, taking a big bite of sandwich.

"If he's with Carly, which he seems to be most of the time these days, we snap his picture and show it to Kate!" Stephanie said.

"Don't you think Kate's probably seen them together already?" I said doubtfully.

"If she's seen them, she hasn't really *seen* them," Stephanie replied. "You can ignore stuff in real life that you just can't in a photograph."

"I don't know," I said uneasily. "Won't that make Kate feel sort of dumb? She might get mad at *us*."

"It seems to me that she'd get madder if she found out that we *didn't* clue her in about Taylor and Carly, wouldn't she?" Stephanie said. "Besides, if you ask me, Kate's crush on Taylor Sprouse is *ruining* her life. It's definitely ruining mine! We've got to save her from herself!" Stephanie always manages to be really convincing, even when her ideas are a little crazy. "Let's go! We'll try the art studio first."

"O-kay . . ." I said reluctantly. We took a short-cut through the gym and pushed against the green door of the art studio. It didn't budge.

"It's locked!" Stephanie said. She knocked on it three or four times. But nobody answered. "Ms. Gilberto?" she called out. Still nothing.

"Nuts!" said Stephanie. "I was sure we'd find Taylor here, and Carly not far behind." She sat down on the bench outside the door and munched thought-fully on her sandwich. "Where could he be?"

"Hanging out at the side entrance?" I suggested. "That's where he was Monday."

"It's worth a try," Stephanie said. She finished her sandwich in two or three bites and wiped her hands on her red corduroy pants, so I choked down my egg salad, too. We were just about to cut through the gym again when we heard voices coming toward us.

"Your last video was very interesting." It was Ms. Gilberto.

"Yes, Taylor," a girl's voice said. "I just loved the part in the empty swimming pool!"

"*Taylor*," Stephanie and I mouthed at each other.

And suddenly there they were! Taylor, Carly, and Ms. Gilberto, stepping through the gym doors.

I have to hand it to Stephanie. She was very speedy. Before even *I* knew what was going on, she whipped Patti's camera out of her tote bag, aimed, and fired! The flash went off practically in their faces. The three of them blinked a few times while Stephanie hurriedly explained, "For the fifth-grade newspaper! Come on, Lauren!"

And we raced away before they could say anything.

"St-Stephanie," I stammered through my giggles, "the newspaper went out of business months ago!"

"I know that, and you know that, but do they know that?" Stephanie said. "Check this out. Every picture sure does tell a story."

She stuck the Polaroid photo, which had just finished developing, under my nose. Ms. Gilberto, Taylor, and Carly all seemed pretty startled. But the important thing was . . . Taylor and Carly were almost holding hands!

"Their fingers are touching!" I squeaked.

"That's what it looks like to me," said Stephanie. "And I think it will to Kate, too."

Chapter
8

But if Stephanie thought the photograph was going to show Kate the light, she was wrong.

Stephanie stuck the picture of Taylor and Carly and Ms. Gilberto into the stack of Polaroids from Bitsy's sleepover. As soon as the final bell rang that afternoon, she swung around in her seat and held the pile of photos out to Kate and me.

"Here we are in the hot tub, remember, Lauren?" Stephanie said.

"Sure. And these are Pumpkin's kittens," I said, taking my cue from her.

Stephanie rearranged the Polaroids again. "Lauren on the exercise bicycle," she said, flipping through them. "And this is . . . ooops! Wrong photo."

But Kate grabbed it to take a closer look. "Ms. Gilberto, Taylor, and Carly," she said coolly. "Great picture of Taylor. And Carly, too." She handed it back to Stephanie without another word!

"I give up," Stephanie muttered to me once we'd joined the crowds in the hall. "Love is blind! And we're doomed! Tomorrow is Lacy Nordstrum's birthday, and Kate will lie on the floor in her rags, and our names will be *mud* with Mrs. Wainwright until we graduate!"

"We could ask Kate not to use any of her special shots," I said.

"She probably wouldn't even hear us," Stephanie said gloomily. "She's in another world. We're definitely done for this time."

Thursday afternoon came all too quickly. Kate dashed out of 5B as soon as the three o'clock bell rang. Her mom was taking her to get her allergy shot before the party started.

As Stephanie, Patti, and I headed down the hall, Mrs. Jamison yodeled over the heads of the other kids, "Lauren-Patti-Stephanie — Mrs. Wainwright wants to see you right away!"

In her office, Mrs. Wainwright told us, "I'm sorry to switch plans on you so late, girls, but Lacy's mother had her dining room painted a few days ago, and for some reason the paint hasn't dried. So the party is moving to my house — Twenty-two Lily Pond Lane."

"No problem," said Stephanie. "We'll be there at four."

"There *might* be a problem," I said as we hurried out toward the bike rack. "We can call Bitsy at home to let her know. But how are we supposed to get in touch with Kate?"

"Phone her doctor, the one who gives her the allergy shots," Patti suggested.

"Dr. Tompkins retired," I said. "The new one's at the hospital, and I don't know his name."

"I'm sure Kate'll go home sometime before the party," Stephanie sighed. "Fix herself up a little, or just the opposite. . . . I'll keep calling her house until I reach her."

But at a quarter to four, when my mom backed her car out of our driveway to take me, as Barkly, to Mrs. Wainwright's, Kate's garage was still empty.

"They're not back yet!" I groaned.

"Maybe they've already come and gone," Mom said. "You know how Kate hates to be late."

"The old Kate hates to be late," I murmured. "Who knows about the new Kate?" But maybe Stephanie *had* caught her at home, and Kate was on her way to the party.

Mrs. Wainwright's house is a small, neat, brick two-story, with a perfect lawn and a little brick garage in back. As Mom let me out at the curb, Stephanie called softly from the front door, "Lauren, did you see Kate?"

I shook my head and dashed up the sidewalk.

"Then we're in big trouble," Stephanie said grimly.

She led me back to the kitchen. Mrs. Wainwright was helping Patti add a comet to her face with yellow sun block. Lacy's mother was touching up the fudge frosting on the huge birthday cake. And Bitsy Barton was crouched in a corner, dividing her time between Whiplash, Mrs. Jamison, and a cardboard box with the two remaining puppies in it.

"What are the puppies and Mrs. Jamison doing here?" I asked.

"Don't ask!" Stephanie said. Then she took a deep breath and told me anyway. "They ate up Mrs. Barton's living-room couch, and Bitsy was afraid her mom might get ideas about the pound if she left them with her. So Biff drove them all over here on his way to Todd's." She lowered her voice. "And Lauren, we need Kate. The video camera is jammed!"

"You're kidding!" I whispered.

"I'm not kidding!" Stephanie said. "I thought I could film the party until we got hold of Kate, but I can't get anything to move! Look!"

She handed the camera to me, but no matter what button I pushed, nothing whirred or clicked.

"Hello, Lauren." Mrs. Wainwright had spotted me. "Where's Kate?"

"Oh . . . uh . . . she'll be here soon," I said, giving the camera back to Stephanie.

"I spoke to Brian Kennan's mother today. She told me about the videotape Kate took at their party," Mrs. Wainwright went on, outlining the yellow tail of a comet across Patti's cheek.

"You gave it to her?" I muttered to Stephanie.

"My mom gave it to her this morning. Mrs. Kennan called to ask where it was, and Mom didn't know about the problem," Stephanie mumbled miserably.

But Mrs. Wainwright was still talking. "Mrs. Kennan thought it was so terrific and original. She said it was *so* clever of Kate to shoot from odd angles. It made the children appear to be floating, as if they were really weightless, at a party in outer space."

"Is that what Kate was doing on the floor?" Stephanie whispered.

"I guess it's possible," I said, sort of impressed.

The kids had started to arrive by then. Mrs. Nordstrum got them settled around the table in the dining room, and soon it was past four o'clock.

"It's time to begin," said Mrs. Wainwright, looking a little worried. "Do you think Kate — "

"Lauren and Patti will tell some of their jokes, Mrs. Wainwright. I'm sure Kate's on her way," Stephanie said. "Get out there, guys," she murmured to us. "I'm going to call Kate again."

Patti and I bounced into the dining room and all the kids clapped and cheered. We shook hands with Lacy — the birthday girl — a thin, little kid with short, straight brown hair, big brown eyes, and a small, shy smile. Then we went into our routine:

Sparkly: "What do Martians have that nobody else has?"

Barkly: "*Woof*. That's easy. *Baby* Martians! *Arf, arf, arf!*"

Big laughs all around. Lacy giggled, and even Mrs. Wainwright grinned.

Barkly: "Now I've got a hard one. How many space monsters will fit into an empty van?"

Sparkly: "Just one. After that, the van isn't empty anymore. Tee-hee-hee."

We'd done four or five space jokes like that when suddenly I heard arguing behind us, from the other side of the swinging door to the kitchen. "We tried to call you, Kate!" Stephanie was insisting.

"Sure you did! You were afraid I'd lie on the floor again, and embarrass you, so you purposely didn't tell me the party had moved!"

"We just found out this afternoon!" Bitsy squeaked.

But Kate ignored her. "We're supposed to be a

team, remember? Some team! If the Nordstrums' neighbor hadn't been outside his house to tell us where the party was, I never would have gotten here!"

Patti and I turned some cartwheels, but I could still hear Kate and Stephanie. "That doesn't happen to be true, Kate Beekman!" Stephanie said, sounding angry now. "But what about you?!" she added in an even louder voice. "You told us that Taylor went to the conference. And we know he *didn't,* because we saw him at the mall!"

"I never said that!" Kate thundered.

"Hey, guys," Bitsy was interrupting nervously. And then her dogs began to bark, maybe because of the yelling, or because of the kids laughing and clapping in the dining room.

Patti and I just happened to have started another joke about then, which went:

Sparkly: "How can you tell a spaceship from a puppy?"

Barkly: "If it wags its tail, it's a puppy!"

Suddenly, the swinging door burst open, and all four dogs — Whiplash, Mrs. Jamison, and the two puppies — came racing into the dining room!

"Puppies!" Lacy squealed, grabbing one of the brown-and-white fur balls. "Mommy, I'm so happy! You got me *puppies* for my birthday!"

I saw Mrs. Nordstrum look at Mrs. Wainwright with raised eyebrows, and then throw her hands up in the air. "I think the puppies have just found themselves a home," I said to Patti. Lacy was hugging one, and Mrs. Nordstrum was stroking the other.

Then Kate and Stephanie had to postpone their argument, because it really was time for Kate to start filming. We closed Mrs. Jamison up in the laundry room, told some more jokes, and Bitsy put Whiplash through his tricks.

Then we turned off the lights and turned on the Barton star maker. There was cake, and candles, and singing, all under the starlight. Lacy opened her presents, still holding a puppy — the smallest one of all. And Kate filmed everything. Sometimes she filmed right-side-up, and sometimes upside-down. She panned and did close ups. And she did it all like such a pro that even Stephanie muttered, "I hate to say this, but maybe she did learn something at that conference. . . ." Even though we were fighting, we were still definitely a team!

Finally the party was over. Mrs. Wainwright thanked us all, told us what a terrific job we'd done, and gave Stephanie a check for forty-five dollars!

Mr. Jenkins loaded us into his van, Bitsy and Whiplash and Mrs. Jamison included. As we headed for home, Patti turned up the radio, and we took up the argument again, under cover of Mr. Jenkins's classical music station.

"What do you mean, you never said Taylor went to the conference?!" Stephanie exclaimed.

"Yeah, you went on and on about how much everybody liked Taylor's video!" I added.

"His *video!*" Kate said. "Taylor sent his tapes to the conference with Ms. Gilberto, but he had to stay in Riverhurst. His grandmother was having some kind of operation."

"So why are you dressing like him? And talking like him and everything," I asked her.

Kate blushed. "Weren't you guys getting a little tired of me the way I was?" she said awkwardly. "I thought maybe I was getting a little dull, and that I should try to act cooler. . . ."

I remembered what Stephanie had said about Kate not being Angela Marx, and how her videotapes wouldn't be any better than Karla Stamos's slides. And we *had* jumped at the chance to go to Bitsy's for a sleepover, hadn't we? "A *new* menu, a *new* house, a *new* family — a total change!" I could just hear Stephanie and me.

"I decided to change my whole act, videotapes included," Kate was saying. "How do you like it?"

I took a deep breath. "I'm sure the new tapes are great," I said, "but I like the old Kate just fine."

"I couldn't agree more," Stephanie said. "And where did you find these awful clothes, anyway?" she added, pointing at Kate's ripped jeans.

Kate grinned. "There was this great shop in the city called Reruns, and I got all this stuff for less than fifteen dollars!"

"The Sleepover Friends Party Service will give you fifteen dollars to throw it out!" said Stephanie firmly.

Kate started to giggle. "It was taking me too long to decide what to wear every morning anyhow," she said.

"It's quite a look," Stephanie said.

"And quite a look on your videotape for the Kennans," Patti said. "Mrs. Kennan told Mrs. Wainwright she loved it!"

"Wait till you see my program for social studies tomorrow," said Kate. "That's what I've been working on with Ms. Gilberto." But she refused to tell us any more about it.

"So you don't like Taylor Sprouse?" I said as Mr. Jenkins turned the corner onto Pine Street. I wanted to get it straight once and for all.

"I like his *videos!*" Kate said. Then she added, "I guess I thought I did like *him* for a while, but that was *months* ago. Anyway, I told you guys Carly Anson likes Taylor."

"So we've noticed," Stephanie said.

Mr. Jenkins put on his brakes and pulled up in front of Kate's house. "Everything okay now?" he turned around to ask us.

"You bet!" said Stephanie.

And Kate and Patti and I said, "All for one and one for all."

Then Patti opened her door to let Kate climb out. Mrs. Jamison took one hard look at the big outdoors and leaped across Patti's legs to freedom!

"Oh! Catch her!" Bitsy yelped. I think it was the first word she'd said since we'd left the Nordstrums'. All of us scrambled out of the van, and raced after Mrs. Jamison.

The dog was making a beeline across Pine Street, straight toward *Mr. Winkler's* house. "Oh, no!" I gasped, because there was the old grouch himself raking leaves in his front yard.

"We've got to grab her before she gets anywhere near him!" I cried.

"He'll call Animal Control!" Patti added — which is just what Mr. Winkler is always threatening to do to Bullwinkle. She hurled herself at Mrs. Jamison just as the dog reached the curb.

But Patti missed, and Mrs. Jamison hopped neatly over the curb, trotted up the sidewalk, and poked Mr. Winkler's leg with her nose.

"Hey, what's going on here?!" Mr. Winkler whirled around to glare at us. After all, Patti and I were still dressed as Sparkly and Barkly. "Is this your dog?" he growled.

"She's . . . she's a stray . . . basically," Bitsy replied in a quavering voice. "C-come on, Mrs. Jamison," she called from outside Mr. Winkler's gate.

"How are you, girl?" Mr. Winkler said to the dog. He reached down to scratch her head, and her tail started wagging a mile a minute. "A stray, is she?"

Stephanie and Kate had caught up with us, so all five of us nodded.

"You know, I've been thinking of getting a dog myself," Mr. Winkler said slowly. "Is she a good watchdog?"

"She's not exactly attack-trained," Stephanie murmured, and she and I got the giggles at the thought of Mrs. Jamison jumping on anybody!

But Kate answered, "Definitely. She barks real loud," which was true — we'd just seen her demonstrate it at the party.

Then Mrs. Jamison rubbed her head against Mr. Winkler's knee, and he actually *smiled!*

"That's a first!" Patti whispered.

"Good girl," Mr. Winkler said. To us he added, "If nobody wants her, I think I'll keep her!"

"You w-will?" said Bitsy, not believing her ears.

"She has very winning ways," said Mr. Winkler. He leaned his rake against a tree. "Come on, sweetheart. I have a leftover lamb chop inside, which should be tasty."

"I don't believe it," Kate said as he led Mrs. Jamison up the front steps and into the house. "Mr. Winkler is a real person after all!"

"And the whole family has found good homes, thanks to you guys!" Bitsy said gratefully. "I really owe you one. Or four."

When I rode to the corner the next morning, Kate was already there. And she looked the way Kate is supposed to look. She was wearing her blue-and-white jacket, and her new pink-and-gray sweats. Her hair was parted in the middle and brushed back on the sides just like it usually is. It was a sight for sore eyes.

The four of us got to school on time, and we also got a big "Hello!" from Mrs. Wainwright, who raved about Kate's birthday video. But that was nothing compared to what happened in class.

Since we were having a test in social studies that afternoon, Mrs. Mead announced that Kate would present her video program just after math was over.

Kate had borrowed the TV with the big screen from the art studio. She popped her videotape into the VCR, adjusted the sound . . . and there she was on the screen. "I'm Kate Beekman," she said, "and this is my day in the city. . . ."

Then there was a whirring sound, and we were suddenly gliding up a city sidewalk, fast. And Henry Larkin shouted from the back of the room, "Hey! She's on roller skates!"

And she was! Kate filmed the whole day on roller skates: She zipped around the museum on them. She even skated into a diner for lunch. We saw all of the famous city sights, the crowded streets, and the huge buildings. And nobody was bored for a second. Kate picked really neat things to focus on, like an old man eating a foot-long hot dog, or a little kid chasing a runaway red balloon! But what made it even better was that we were seeing all the bumps and bobbles that came from Kate being on skates! We were even part of her crash landing when she skated over a big crack in the pavement and fell flat on her rear end.

The class absolutely loved it. They applauded for at least five minutes. For me, though, the end was the best. The screen went black, and then Kate's voice said, "This program is dedicated to my best friends, Lauren, Patti, and Stephanie."

Sleepover Friends forever!

#27 Where's Patti?

"Lau-ren!" Stephanie said crossly, lurching to a halt.

"We have to talk," I said so seriously that Stephanie didn't make me explain myself, for once.

"Okay," she agreed. She turned to the tall seventh-grader she'd been dancing with. "Thanks for the dance, Andrew."

"Don't you think he's cute? *I* do!" she whispered to me as she followed me off the dance floor. "Did you have to cut in? I was having fun!"

"Sorry," I said, pushing her onto a folding chair and flopping down next to her. "But it's important. Have you seen Patti?"

Pack your bags for fun and adventure with

SLEEPOVER FRIENDS™
by Susan Saunders